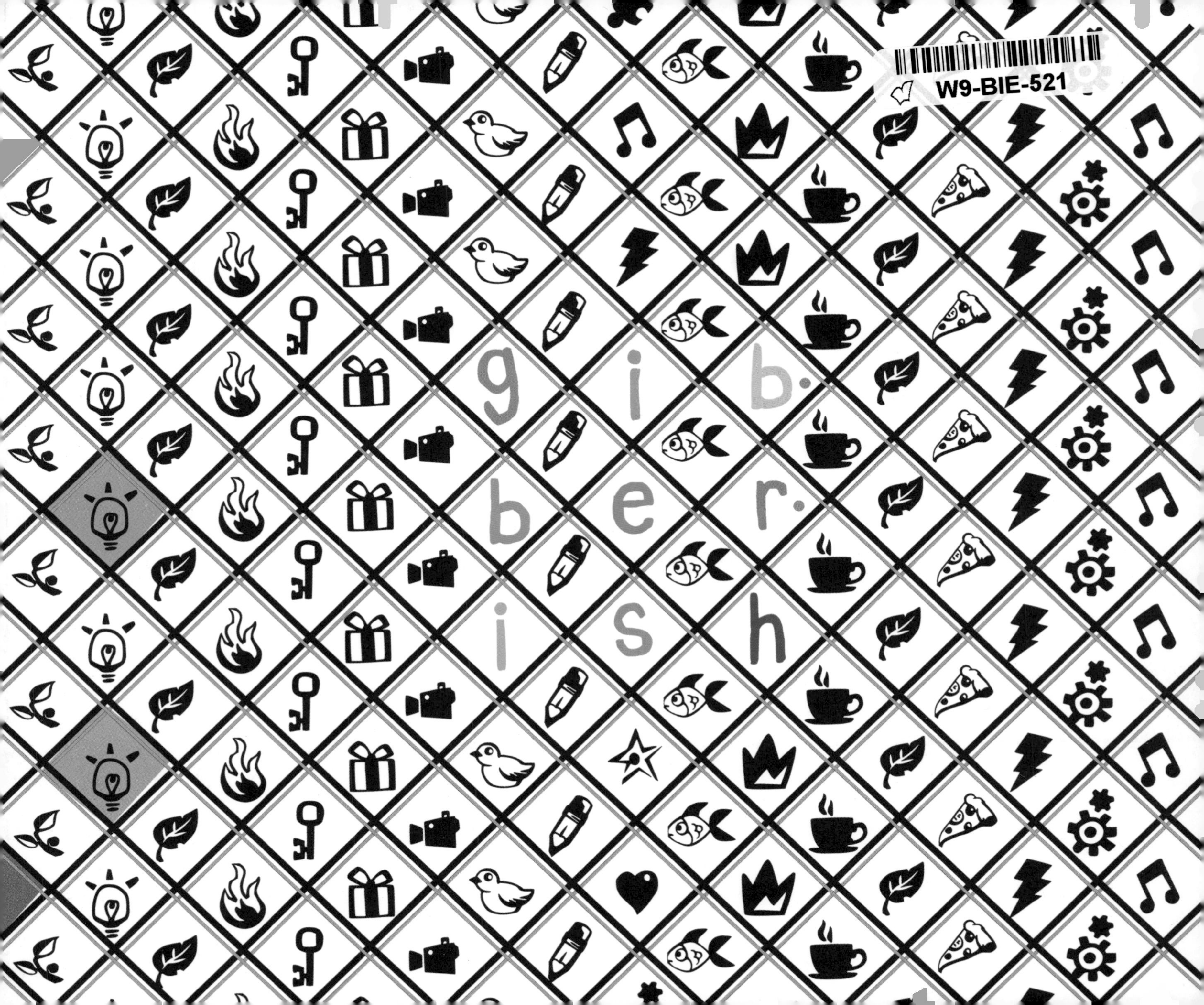
gibberish

Gib·ber·ish

by YOUNG VO

LQ
LEVINE QUERIDO
MONTCLAIR • AMSTERDAM • HOBOKEN

This is an Arthur A. Levine book
Published by Levine Querido

LQ
LEVINE QUERIDO

www.levinequerido.com · info@levinequerido.com

Levine Querido is distributed by Chronicle Books, LLC

Library of Congress Cataloging-in-Publication data is available
ISBN 978-1-64614-110-4

Printed and bound in China

MIX
Paper | Supporting responsible forestry
FSC www.fsc.org
FSC™ C104723

Published in February 2022
Fifth Printing

Book design by Patrick Collins
The text type was set in Billy Bold.

Young Vo began the artwork for this picture book
with pencil sketches, which grew into colored pencils,
and then watercolor. It became a big, fun mess of mixed media,
cleaned up digitally in Clip Studio Paint and Adobe Photoshop.

For Kelly Thuy Troung
who took me to a brighter place

First Dat sailed on a boat,

then flew on a plane,

and today Dat will be on a school bus.

"When people speak it will sound like gibberish, Dat.

Just listen, and do the best you can," Mah said.

"Hello, my name is Dat."

In gibberish, the bus driver said,

Dat nodded. But he didn't really understand.

The teacher said,
Dan.

In class, everyone knew gibberish

except for Dat.

Gibberish was in the books and in the air.

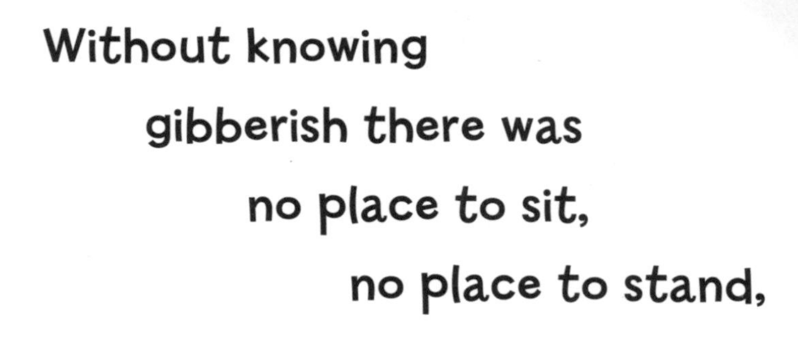

Without knowing
gibberish there was
no place to sit,
no place to stand,

and no one to play with.

So Dat walked.

"Hello, my name is Dat."

Then...

something
unexpected
fell
from
a
tree.

"Hi, my name is Dat."
"I'm not sure
what you're saying."

Back in the classroom,
Dat tried to read,
but his words **broke.**

T nOW jum
O ε he o

The last school bell rang
and it was time to go home.

On the bus ride Dat sat alone.

Then...

someone

unexpected

dropped

in.

Dat began to hear words.

Tree

boat
duck
book
frog
flower

home
plane
ball
Julie

HA
Dat!
HA

Julie, you know my name!
HA
HA
HA
HA
HA

Mah, I'm back.

Hi.
This is my friend, Julie.
Dat.
Hi, Dat.

Dat flew on a plane,
Dat sailed on a boat,
Dat rode on a school bus,
and today Dat ran home
with Julie.